ALONSO

TAKES THE STAGE

REBEL GiRLS

Our books are available at special quantity discounts for bulk purchase for sale promotions, premiums, fundraising, and educational needs. For details, write to sales@rebelgirls.com

Art Director: Giulia Flamini
Text: Nancy Ohlin
Cover and Illustrations: Josefina Preumayr
Cover Lettering: Cesar Yannarella
Graphic Design: Annalisa Ventura

This is a work of historical fiction. We have tried to be as accurate as possible, but names, characters, businesses, places, events, locales, and incidents may have been changed to suit the needs of the story.

www.rebelgirls.com
Printed in China

ISBN 978-1-7333292-2-4

MIX
From responsible sources
FSC® C124807

MORE BOOKS
FROM REBEL GIRLS . . .

Good Night Stories for Rebel Girls

•

Good Night Stories for Rebel Girls 2

•

I Am a Rebel Girl:

A Journal to Start Revolutions

•

Ada Lovelace Cracks the Code

•

Madam C. J. Walker Builds a Business

•

Junko Tabei Masters the Mountains

•

Dr. Wangari Maathai Plants a Forest

To the Rebel Girls of the world...

Follow your own rhythm
and the world will dance along.

Alicia Alonso
December 21, 1920-October 17, 2019
Cuba

A licia's father strolled into the living room, settled into his favorite rocking chair, and loosened his tie. "Let's begin, shall we? Ernestina, why don't you go first? The rest of you can follow after your mother."

Alicia was excited. It was time for the family talent show!

She loved this nightly tradition, how they gathered after dinner to perform for one another—everyone except Papá, who was always an audience member. They performed dances, songs, skits, comedy routines, and more. There was usually no rehearsing ahead of time.

I will do a dance tonight, Alicia thought,

nodding to herself. Of course, she almost always danced for the talent show. Dancing was her very favorite activity in the world.

She had a few minutes to come up with a magnificent performance outfit. Last night, she'd worn her father's black top hat and her mother's gloves—one lace, one leather. Tonight, she would try a different look.

She raced into the hallway, paused at the linen closet, and grabbed a bath towel, which could be draped over her short dark hair like a *mantilla*. And what about the silk curtains in the dining room? She could turn them into a swirly skirt to wear over her stiff taffeta dress…although Maria, the family's maid, might not appreciate her using them for a costume again. Instead, Alicia grabbed a couple of white linen napkins that might be useful.

Back in the living room, Mamá had taken her place next to Papá. She leafed through a thick volume of poetry, looking for the perfect poem to recite. Alicia plopped down on the velvet settee next to her sister, Blanca, and waited. Outside the window, the twilit sky bloomed pink and purple. In the distance, the lights of downtown Havana winked like stars. A warm breeze carried the smell of salt water from the nearby bay.

Mamá pointed to a page in her poetry book. "This one!" she announced. She touched the emerald brooch at her throat and began reading in a slow, clear voice. It wasn't a children's poem, and Alicia, who was six, didn't understand all the words. Still, she loved the way her mother recited the lines…sometimes quietly, and other times loudly and dramatically. Mamá was like an actress!

Alicia's teenage brothers, Antonio and Elizardo, went next. They took off their suit jackets, which Papá always made them wear at dinner, and rolled up their shirtsleeves. They sang a lively duet about sailors on the sea. When they finished, nine-year-old Blanca performed one of her famous

humming numbers. Alicia's sister was a genius at humming.

Finally, it was Alicia's turn. She took her position in front of the bookshelves. She fastened the bath towel over her neatly combed hair and let it cascade down her back. She clasped a white linen dinner napkin in each hand. Then she narrowed her large brown eyes in a mysterious way.

"Music, please!" she said grandly.

"Of course." Mamá smiled and walked over to the record player. She chose something from a shelf full of records, set it on the turntable, and lowered the needle. The needle made a fuzzy, scratchy sound as it bounced on the disc. Then it settled, and a song began to play.

Conga drums. Guitars. Violins. A bandoneon. Alicia recognized the song; it was by one of her mother's favorite Cuban bands. She closed her eyes and let the music wash over her. Upbeat... downbeat...*now!*

Her eyes flew open as she raised her arms in the air. She flapped the dinner napkins like furious little hummingbird wings. She stomped her feet on the tiled floor in time with the conga drums. She twirled on the wave of a mournful bandoneon note, and her bath-towel mantilla twirled along with her.

She knew that her family was watching her, but she wasn't watching them back. She was happily lost in her flapping and stomping and twirling. According to Mamá and Papá, she'd been doing this practically since she could walk—bursting into dance whenever she heard music and disappearing into her own world.

At the moment, her world was the conga beat of the song and the swift, shimmering movements of her body.

The violins came in, their melody swaying back and forth. Alicia swayed with them. The guitars joined in, thrumming rapidly like raindrops.

Alicia thrummed with them. No one had taught her how to dance. The moves came naturally, from somewhere deep within her.

When she was done, she curtsied.

"Brava!" Mamá and Papá cried out.

"Brava!" Blanca and Antonio and Elizardo joined in.

"Muchas gracias!" Alicia replied.

She curtsied again, holding on to her bath-towel mantilla to keep it from sliding awkwardly down her head. For a moment, she imagined that she was on a real stage, blinking into the spotlights as a whole auditorium full of people clapped and cheered.

Maybe someday?

CHAPTER TWO

The following year, in 1928, Alicia's family moved to Spain for ten months for her father's work. He was a veterinarian who specialized in horses, and the government of Cuba had sent him to find some for the Cuban army. Spain was known for its fine horses that were a mix of Spanish, English, and Arab breeds.

Alicia liked a lot of things about Spain—the lively crowds, the flamenco music drifting out of cafés, the markets selling colorful clothes and pretty combs. But she *loved* her weekly lesson at Señora Vega's dance studio. Mamá had signed her and Blanca up to learn some traditional dances. That way, they could surprise their Spanish-born grandfather with a little recital when they moved back home in the spring.

This week's lesson was learning sevillanas.

"One, two, three, four, five, six," Señora Vega counted as Alicia and Blanca practiced the sevillanas steps. "Muy bueno, Alicia! Blanca, remember to begin lifting your arm on *five* and then finish lifting on *six* to correspond with your foot movements. Okay, let's run through it again. This time with music!"

"Sí, Señora Vega!" Alicia and Blanca replied.

As Señora Vega cued the music on a record player, the sisters rushed back to the middle of the studio floor and assumed the sevillanas starting position: feet together, arms low and curved.

"We look like we're holding giant invisible pumpkins," Blanca whispered to Alicia, giggling.

Alicia grinned but didn't reply. She was busy studying her reflection in the window.

She wanted to make sure that her posture was

straight, the way Señora Vega had shown them, and that her head was angled just so, with her chin lifted proudly.

"What are you, the queen of the pumpkins?" Blanca teased.

"Very funny!" Alicia giggled but kept her pose. She wanted to learn this dance perfectly.

Guitar music started to play. The girls fell silent and faced forward.

Señora Vega sauntered toward them, clapping to the beat.

"Four, five, six, *begin*! Right foot, tap in place… left foot forward…right foot touch…right foot back…left foot touch…stand still! Now repeat on the other side! *Left* foot, tap in place…right foot forward…left foot touch…"

Señora Vega continued calling out instructions. But Alicia didn't really need them. Even though it was only her first sevillanas lesson, she had pretty much memorized the choreography for her feet.

She learned the arm positions, too, and her arms floated up and down in sync with the music.

From the record player, the snapping and clacking sound of castanets joined the other instruments. Alicia loved the castanets' fierce, confident rhythm and how it made her body feel fierce and confident, too.

They ran through the first *copla*, or section, a few more times, then stopped to take a break.

"Would you young ladies like me to teach you how to play the castanets?" Señora Vega asked. "I have some in the studio."

"Yes, please!" Alicia said immediately.

"Is it hard?" Blanca asked.

"Not if you practice."

Señora Vega reached into a basket for two pairs of castanets. With their shell-shaped lids connected by a hinge, they resembled big clams. They were made of a dark hardwood and had loops of string attached to them.

Señora Vega showed the sisters how to slip the loops over their thumbs.

"Is this right?" Alicia held up her castanets. The wood felt smooth and cool in her hands.

"Yes, exactly! To make the sounds, snap the shells shut and then let go. Snap, let go... Snap, let go... Snap, let go!"

Alicia and Blanca snapped and let go three times. *Clack, clack, clack!*

Maravilloso! Alicia thought.

She kept snapping and letting go, over and over again. Her feet stomped along with the clacks. They moved in a slow, sweeping circle as the stomps and clacks continued.

At five o'clock, Mamá arrived at the studio to pick them up. Blanca was in the corner practicing sevillanas arm positions with Señora Vega. Alicia was still dancing and snapping her castanets.

"Olé, Mamá!" Alicia said with a stomp.

"Olé, Alicia! It's time to go home, mijas."

"Five more minutes... *Pleeeeease?*" Alicia begged.

"Your father is waiting for us back at the house."

"Okay, *three* more minutes, then!"

Mamá chuckled. "How about two?"

"Two and a half!"

Ten minutes later, Mamá and Blanca finally managed to drag Alicia out of the dance studio.

~

That night as Alicia helped her mother prepare dinner, she came up with an excellent plan.

"Mamá? Can I keep taking dance lessons when we go back to Cuba?"

"I don't know of any dance teachers back home," Mamá said, handing her a bowl of olives. "Chop these for me, please."

"Can you find one, then?"

"I can try."

Alicia popped one of the bright green olives into her mouth. "I want to study dancing! It's so much better than reading or writing or arithmetic or anything else!" She thought about her private school in Havana, which was run by nuns. Her classes there were not interesting *at all.*

"School is important, Alicia. Otherwise, how will you marry into a good family someday?" Mamá pointed out.

Alicia scrunched up her face. She had no idea what school had to do with marriage.

"Okay, fine, I'll keep going to regular school. But I want to dance, too!"

"I'll ask some of my friends," her mother said with a sigh. "Maybe they know of a teacher."

Alicia threw her arms around her mother's waist and hugged her tightly. "Thank you, thank you!"

"You're welcome. Now, let's finish cooking, or we'll be eating dinner at midnight!"

Alicia picked up a small knife and chopped the olives slowly and carefully, just like Mamá had taught her to do. As she chopped, her feet tapped

along, and in her head, she counted out a sevillanas beat. *One, two, three, four, five, six, repeat!*

Alicia never wanted to stop dancing. And why should she, when it was so much fun? Alicia knew some Cuban dances already, and she was learning Spanish dances now. She wondered if there were other styles of dancing from other countries that she could learn.

Just then, she noticed some empty clamshells in the sink; Mamá had shucked them and was simmering the clam pieces in wine and garlic. Alicia stopped what she was doing and reached over for a couple of clamshells.

"Olé!" she said, snapping and clacking.

Mamá laughed and shook her head.

CHAPTER THREE

A licia glanced worriedly at the clock in the lobby of the Pro Arte Musical building. Her mother had kept her promise and found a dance teacher in Havana. But Alicia really had to stop daydreaming about dancing if she wanted to get to class on time and *actually dance!*

Señor Yavorsky is going to be mad at me! Alicia thought, breaking into a run. This was the second— no, *third* time she'd been late for class this month.

"Alicia!" Leonor, Alicia's friend and classmate, called to her and waved.

Alicia stopped at Leonor's side. "Hi! Did Señor Yavorsky send you out here to look for me?" she asked breathlessly.

"What? No! I was dying to tell you about the new ballet shoes. Everyone's trying them on!"

Alicia blinked, confused. They usually danced in tennis shoes or in their stocking feet.

"What new ballet shoes?"

"Someone brought a pair back from Italy. They're beautiful! All the girls are trying them on. Whoever fits into them gets to keep them."

"*Wow!*" Alicia exclaimed. She wondered what these special ballet shoes would look like. And she hoped they'd fit her.

"They were too big for me. You should try them on, though."

"I will!"

Alicia flung her bag over her shoulder and hurried to the studio. This was the most exciting thing that had ever happened in ballet class!

Two years ago, in Spain, when she'd told her mother that she wanted to continue with dance lessons back home, Alicia hadn't been thinking about ballet. She hadn't even known what ballet *was*.

Alicia's mother was involved with Pro Arte Musical, a community center that offered concerts and other cultural events. They had also always planned to offer children's drama, music, and dance classes there, but while she and the others in charge had found drama and music teachers for the program, finding a dance instructor had proved difficult. There was no one like Señora Vega in Cuba. The only available teacher turned out to be Nikolai Yavorsky, a ballet dancer from Russia. So it was to be ballet or nothing.

Luckily, Alicia fell in love with this new dance style—new to Cuba, anyway—from her very first plié. She loved being able to tell stories and express emotions through the graceful movements. She loved the elegant classical music from Europe, too.

In fact, she loved ballet so much that she was

thinking about becoming a professional ballerina when she grew up! She hadn't told Mamá or Papá or anyone else yet, but the idea of it felt so right. So *Alicia.*

And luckily for her, ballet technique came as naturally to her as did the traditional Spanish dances she'd learned in Señora Vega's studio. Well, *almost* as naturally. Ballet technique was difficult. But because she enjoyed it so much, Alicia didn't mind.

As Alicia rushed into the practice room, a dozen girls sat in a circle on the gleaming wood floor. A girl named Sofia was trying to squeeze her foot into a pink satin shoe with ribbons dangling from it.

Señor Yavorsky stood at the barre, watching. "These shoes are called 'pointe shoes' because they enable the dancer to stand *en pointe*, which is French for 'on the tips of the toes,'" he explained to the class. "This is en pointe"—he lifted his right heel and then the ball of his foot until he was on the tips of his right toes—"except you do it with both feet at the same time."

"Too small," Sofia said, pouting. She passed the pointe shoes to the next girl.

Alicia joined the circle. Her teacher raised his eyebrows at her and tapped his watch. She mouthed, *I'm sorry!*

Eventually, it was Alicia's turn to try on the pointe shoes. They'd been too big or too small for everyone else.

Captivated, Alicia turned them over in her hands. She'd never seen shoes like these before. They were smooth and stiff, and the toe parts were hard and boxy. The satin was shiny, and the color reminded her of the pale pink roses in her mother's garden.

Alicia slipped her right foot into one pointe shoe, then her left foot into the other. She wriggled her toes in the boxy part. She wasn't sure what to

do with the dangling ribbons, though.

A girl named Beatriz leaned over and criss-crossed them over Alicia's shins. "Like this," she explained, tying the ends into neat bows.

"Thank you!"

Alicia stood up slowly, slowly. She lifted herself up onto the very tips of her toes, the way Señor Yavorsky had demonstrated—except that she did it with both feet.

I'm standing on my toes!

Balancing carefully, she took a few steps en pointe, making a soft *clunk, clunk, clunk* along the wood floor. The shoes fit perfectly. But her feet quickly grew tired from holding themselves up like that, so she lowered them and resumed walking normally.

"The shoes seem to fit, Alicia. I guess they belong to you now," Señor Yavorsky told her.

Alicia felt like Cinderella. More importantly, she felt like a real ballerina!

During class, Alicia did her barre exercises in her new shoes: first position, plié…second position, plié…all the way through to fifth position. She did her floor exercises in them, too: run, jeté, land and then the delicate little cat steps—pas de chat, pas de chat, pas de chat. The stiff, boxy construction of the shoes made the muscles in her feet ache, and she could feel blisters forming. But she didn't care. She never wanted to take them off!

Throughout class, Señor Yavorsky strolled around and corrected everyone's postures and movements as he always did, calling out orders like "Straighten those legs!" and "Hold in your stomachs!" and "Necks up, shoulders down!" He was a tough teacher, and he ran his studio in a strict way.

But after class, he often showed a softer side. He liked to tell stories about the ballet stars from his home country.

Today, as the girls put on their coats and street

shoes and prepared to go home, he spoke to them about a ballerina he knew named Anna Pavlova.

"She was as light as a feather when she danced," he said, staring dreamily across the room as though Pavlova might appear there. "She was so expressive, too! Audiences wept when they saw her in *The Dying Swan*, which was a short ballet created especially for her. With her movements, she was able to transform herself into a beautiful swan fighting tragically for its life." He sighed. "Pavlova was and always will be one of the greatest ballerinas in history! Perhaps *the* greatest! Make no mistake, she had to work very hard to achieve all this. She was a small, frail child, and she had weak, thin ankles. But she practiced! She took extra lessons! She was determined to become the best, and she did just that."

Alicia clutched her pointe shoes in her hands— she didn't want to put them away in her bag just yet—and leaned forward to listen intently to her teacher. She imagined a young girl with her small, frail body and weak, thin ankles practicing and taking extra lessons and growing stronger, more nimble. Then she imagined that girl grown-up, dancing on grand stages all over the world, moving the crowd to tears and thunderous applause.

If Anna Pavlova could work hard to become one of the greatest ballerinas in history, maybe Alicia could do the same?

~

Later that week, as Alicia got ready for bed, she overheard her parents talking quietly about her in the hallway.

"She won't take off those pink ballet shoes of hers," Papá was saying. "She greets me at the door in them when I get home from work. I think she sleeps with them, too."

Alicia glanced across her room. The pointe

shoes were on her pillow next to her teddy bear. Where they belonged. She kept them close, and they helped her have the most wonderful dreams about ballet!

"Alicia *does* love her ballet classes," Mamá replied. "She's even dropped her drama classes at Pro Arte Musical so that she can focus on ballet."

"As long as it's just a passing phase. I will not have my daughter becoming a professional dancer."

"No, of course not."

Alicia frowned. Why "of course not"? Didn't her parents realize that she might be a future ballet star?

She turned out the lights, climbed into bed, and hugged her ballet shoes close as she fell asleep. She hoped she would have a dream about her stage debut. Would it be one of the dances her teacher had told her about, like *The Dying Swan*? Or some other ballet altogether?

CHAPTER FOUR

A licia's stage debut eventually happened at Señor Yavorsky's studio recital in December 1931. The recital consisted of lots of different dances from different ballets. Alicia was in a small ensemble dance, and she loved being onstage in front of an audience!

The following year, Alicia danced onstage again, this time in a production of the *Sleeping Beauty* ballet. She was assigned the part of the bluebird, which involved lots of difficult jumping and spinning and fluttering. Afterward, Señor Yavorsky told her that she had become one of his best pupils, which made her want to jump and spin and flutter for joy!

Alicia continued to practice and take extra classes, yet ballet never felt like work to her. It had become the center of her universe, and she loved it so much that she was only truly happy when she was dancing. She spent every free minute she had at Pro Arte Musical. She rarely saw her school friends. She gave up her other hobbies, like roller skating and horseback riding, because she was worried about getting hurt and having to miss her ballet classes. And when she wasn't dancing, she was usually at home reading books about dance.

When Alicia was thirteen, she was cast as one of the leads in a ballet called *Coppélia*. She danced the part of Swanilda, a young woman who was in love with a young man named Franz, who in turn was in love with a doll named Coppélia.

A dancer named Alberto Alonso danced the role of Franz. Alberto was the son of Laura Rayneri de Alonso, the new head of Pro Arte Musical. There had been some big changes since Señora Rayneri took over. For example, there were boys in the ballet classes now, like Alberto.

The opening night of *Coppélia* was a huge success. After the finale, the audience burst into wild applause. Someone threw a bouquet of flowers onto the stage. Alberto scooped it up and gave it to Alicia. She clasped it to her chest as she curtsied. What a magical night!

Friends and family members came backstage to congratulate Alicia and Alberto and the other cast members. One of them happened to be Alberto's older brother, Fernando. He was tall and handsome, with thick dark hair and warm brown eyes.

"Your dancing was beautiful," Fernando said to Alicia as they shook hands. "You were perfect in that role."

"Thank you! I tried to make myself *become* Swanilda in my head," Alicia babbled excitedly. "Who was she, what was she like? After that, the movements came easily. They were Swanilda's movements, not mine."

"That sounds like a very artistic approach," Fernando remarked. "Say...I don't know if you remember me, but we've met before. I came by your house once to see your brother Antonio, but it was ages ago now. You answered the door wearing your ballet shoes and standing on your toes, with your arms like *this*." Fernando raised his own arms above his head in fifth position.

"Oh!"

Alicia blushed and buried her face in her bouquet. It was embarrassing to think that he'd seen her during that phase in her life, when she'd been a silly little girl obsessed with ballet. Of course, she was *still* obsessed with ballet. She just wasn't silly anymore.

Alicia lowered the bouquet to her side and stood a little straighter. "I think I do remember you," she said. "You gave Antonio a ride to a party."

"Yes, that's right! How is Antonio doing, by the way? I haven't seen him in a while."

"He's annoying. But he's fine, I guess."

Fernando laughed.

Alberto ambled up to them and threw his arm around his brother's shoulders. "So? What did you think of the performance?"

"Speaking of annoying brothers…" Fernando whispered to Alicia with a wink. Alicia giggled.

"Alicia was fantastic. You were awful," Fernando teased Alberto.

"Funny! Maybe *you* should take ballet lessons, too, and we can see who's the better dancer."

"Ballet lessons. Hmm…" Fernando smiled at Alicia. "Maybe I will."

"You should! Ballet is *amazing*," Alicia said eagerly. "I plan to be a professional ballerina someday," she added.

"I have no doubt that you will become very famous. And I can tell everyone that I knew you way back when," Fernando told her.

"Well, if you take lessons, maybe you'll become a professional ballerina, too. I mean, ballet *dancer*. You're a boy, so…"

Alicia blushed again. Why was she blushing so much? Fernando made her feel a bit awkward. But in a good way. What was *that* about?

CHAPTER FIVE

True to his word, Fernando began taking lessons with Señor Yavorsky, and he grew to love ballet almost as much as Alicia did. Over the years, the two of them danced in many performances together, and they became some of the brightest stars in the studio.

Fernando also grew to love Alicia, and she loved him back. They were a perfect pair on and off the stage. Alicia had never been so happy.

One evening after a ballet rehearsal, Alicia and Fernando took a walk through a neighborhood called Old Havana. They admired the fine old buildings and the cobblestoned plaza as they strolled hand in hand.

Alicia had seen these buildings and plazas a million times before. But with Fernando, everything seemed fresh and new and beautiful.

"Havana is so pretty, isn't it?" Alicia said dreamily. "I wish we could stay here forever."

"You want to leave?" Fernando asked.

"I worry that we might be outgrowing it," Alicia said, her voice tinged with sadness. "We've learned everything we can from Señor Yavorsky. I feel like we need new mentors. But there aren't any other ballet teachers in Havana."

Fernando stopped in front of Fuente de los Leones, a fountain surrounded by four stone lions. He turned to face her, his eyes bright with excitement.

"I've been thinking about this, too," he said. "And I think I have a solution."

"You do?"

"Yes. What if we moved to America?"

Alicia laughed. *"America?"*

"I was thinking about New York City."

"New York City…" she repeated, imagining what an adventure that would be.

"Just think about it, Alicia! There's so much happening there around dance! George Balanchine, the famous Russian choreographer—"

"Señor Yavorsky told us a story about him once," Alicia recalled.

"Yes! Balanchine has moved to New York to start a dance company called the School of American Ballet. Everyone's talking about it! And if not that one, New York has lots of other dance companies. Cuba has *none*."

Alicia's head was spinning. Fernando was onto something—and to be honest, she'd had her own fantasies about going abroad to study ballet. Alberto, Fernando's brother, had recently moved to Paris to join the Ballet Russe de Monte Carlo. Why shouldn't she and Fernando follow in his footsteps and leave Havana behind, expand their horizons?

Still, their lives and their families were *here*. And what would their teacher say?

"Wouldn't Señor Yavorsky be upset with us?" she asked Fernando.

"I think he would encourage us to go, just as he did with Alberto. He knows we need to grow as dancers to reach the next level."

"Well, then…what would our parents say? Especially *my* parents?"

"We'll have to have a long conversation with them. Hopefully, they'll understand."

Alicia considered this. Mamá had always been supportive of her dancing. She'd even sewn tutus for Alicia and the other girls in the studio. Papá, on the other hand, had never taken her dancing seriously. He still thought of it as a "passing phase." He didn't believe professional dancing was proper for a young woman of Alicia's social class. She disagreed, of course, but it was hard to convince him otherwise. Maybe by moving abroad, she could escape his negative attitude and shape her own destiny, become the ballerina she had always longed to be?

In the distance, Alicia could see the beach and the dark waters of the bay. Somewhere beyond was America. New York City.

Fernando whispered in her ear.

"What?" Alicia asked, not quite sure she'd heard him correctly.

"We could get married," he repeated.

"What?"

Fernando grinned. Then he got down on one knee in front of the fountain, took her hand in his, and kissed it tenderly. "Will you, Alicia Ernestina de la Caridad del Cobre Martínez y del Hoyo, be my wife and move to America with me?"

Alicia began to laugh and cry at the same time. People passing through the plaza stared curiously at them. It seemed as though the four stone lions perched on the fountain were watching them, too.

But she didn't care. The moment was just for her and Fernando.

Of course she belonged with him. No one understood her love of dance the way he did. And he was right that they belonged in New York City. Together.

She nodded through her laughter and tears. "Yes! And yes!"

Their future was set. Alicia couldn't wait!

~

"You can still change your mind," Mamá said as Alicia packed her clothes into a brown leather travel trunk.

Alicia shook her head. "I won't, Mamá." Alicia and Fernando had recently married, and she was getting ready to move to the United States.

"New York City is so far away."

"I promise we'll visit."

Mamá sat down on the edge of Alicia's bed and

twisted her hands in her lap. Her face was lined with worry. Alicia knew that her mother had spent weeks trying to convince Papá to let her live in America with Fernando, even though she herself wasn't crazy about the idea. Papá had finally given in, although he was still not happy about it.

Fernando was already in New York. He'd gotten a job dancing with Mikhail Mordkin's ballet company, and he was waiting for Alicia to join him. She'd received postcards from him with images of Central Park, the Statue of Liberty, and the Empire State Building. The city looked exciting but also very different from Havana.

Alicia reached for her favorite white silk blouse and tried to fold it. But the thin, delicate fabric slipped through her fingers. She tried again, with no success.

"Here." Mamá took the blouse from her, laid it down on the bed, and folded it neatly.

"Gracias, Mamá."

"You'll learn these things, mijita. You'll be in charge of your own household soon."

Alicia gulped. *Her own household.* She'd known this fact in her mind, but the reality of it was only now starting to sink in.

She was still so young, and yet she was about to board a ship bound north for America, to a new life and a new home and a new husband. And a new career. She would not have Mamá or the rest of her family to help with any of it. She had to be an adult now.

I can do this, she told herself. *I can make my own way.*

CHAPTER SIX

The living room in Alicia and Fernando's New York City apartment was much smaller than her family's back in Havana. Sometimes, reminiscing about her childhood, Alicia tried to picture Mamá, Antonio, Elizardo, Blanca, and herself here, dancing and singing and reading poems to Papá as he sat contentedly in his rocking chair. But there was barely enough space in her new home for a rocking chair, much less a makeshift stage.

Still, Alicia—now Alicia Alonso—practiced her dance steps in that tiny living room every day. Sometimes, she danced with Fernando. Sometimes, she danced by herself. She continued to do ballet, but she also practiced Spanish and Cuban dances, like sevillanas and rumba and salsa. She'd even brought her castanets from home, although she tried not to play them too loudly, in case the neighbors complained. Likewise with her foot stomping!

Outside, snow fell and blanketed the busy, bustling street in white. The climate in Cuba was too warm for it to snow, and Alicia was fascinated by the wintry weather. She put a record on the record player—"Waltz of the Snowflakes" from the *Nutcracker* ballet—and began to make up her own steps to go with the lovely, lilting music. As she eyed the snowflakes falling outside, she tried to imitate their movements. With quick, light feet and gently fluttering arms, she transformed herself into a fluffy snowflake swirling and whirling in the winter wind.

Church bells chimed from somewhere in the neighborhood. It was six o'clock, and Fernando

would be home soon. He was busy rehearsing and performing with Mordkin's ballet. Alicia was eager to be hired by an American ballet company, too, but it would have to wait a little while longer. She and Fernando were expecting a baby.

~

"Where did you learn how to dance? You are quite exceptional," Enrico Zanfretta told Alicia. The seventy-year-old ballet teacher leaned on his cane as he looked over her arabesque. Her right leg was extended behind her and perfectly turned out while she balanced on her left leg. Her arms were lifted gracefully to the side and to the front.

Alicia eased out of her arabesque, toweled off her face, and smiled at Mr. Zanfretta. She was still learning English, but just like dancing, she knew she would only improve with practice. "I studied ballet in Havana. Where I used to live," she replied.

"If you keep studying and practicing, you could become a great ballerina."

Alicia beamed. She'd begun taking lessons with Mr. Zanfretta shortly after the baby was born—Laura, named after Fernando's mother. The lessons cost twenty-five cents each, which was a lot of money for Alicia and Fernando. They were no longer the privileged young children of wealthy Cuban families, but newlyweds and new parents trying to make it on their own in a foreign country. Alicia was determined to succeed, though.

So while Fernando rehearsed and performed and toured with the Mordkin's ballet company, Alicia left Laurita, as she was called, with friends and neighbors when she studied with Mr. Zanfretta. He was well-known for training many famous ballet dancers. Alicia planned to audition for ballet companies—or maybe one of the big ballet schools, as a stepping stone—as soon as she felt she was ready.

Then, in 1938, her ballet journey took an unexpected turn.

After Fernando's work with Mordkin's ballet company was over, he found his next job in a musical called *Three Waltzes*. This was not ballet but musical theater. It was an entirely different style of dance.

Alicia sometimes accompanied Fernando to rehearsals for *Three Waltzes*; she loved being around other dancers, even if she wasn't in the production. One day on the set, the dance director, Marjorie Fielding, happened to see Alicia dancing with Fernando as she helped him rehearse a number.

Alicia noticed the dance director noticing her. She smiled and executed a flashy pirouette. Ms. Fielding laughed. When Fernando went to speak to the pianist, she walked over to Alicia.

"Impressive," Ms. Fielding told Alicia. "You are very talented. Where did you study dance?"

"In Havana. And I've been taking lessons here, too. With Mr. Zanfretta," Alicia replied.

"Well, it shows. And we could use another talented dancer in the cast. How would you like to join our little show?"

"Me?"

"Yes, you! I could choreograph a special dance number just for you, to show off your skills."

Alicia considered this. It was not ballet, but it *was* a job in dance—her very first one!

"Yes, I would love that. Thank you!" she replied. She and Ms. Fielding shook hands.

And so *Three Waltzes* became Alicia's American dance debut. The shows took place at an enormous

open-air stadium at Jones Beach, just outside
New York City, in front of a massive audience
of more than ten thousand people. Dressed in
a white chiffon gown, Alicia danced with two
male partners. The number Ms. Fielding had
choreographed for her was an elegant waltz with
lots of complicated turns and lifts.

After *Three Waltzes*, Alicia was cast in other
musical theater productions, and so was Fernando.
Musical theater involved even more storytelling
than ballet, and Alicia had always been good at
understanding the characters she portrayed, like
Swanilda in *Coppélia*, and using movements and
facial expressions to tell their stories.

But Alicia still dreamed of becoming a
professional ballerina. Would it ever happen? Had
she and Fernando made a mistake by coming to
America?

Be patient, she told herself.

And then came her big ballet break.

CHAPTER SEVEN

I n 1939, Alicia auditioned to study at the School of American Ballet. SAB was the school that Fernando had mentioned to her back in Havana, the one cofounded by the famous Russian dancer and choreographer George Balanchine.

When the letter came in the mail saying that she'd been accepted *and* that she would receive a scholarship to pay for her tuition, she danced around her and Fernando's tiny living room.

"Yes! I'm going to become a professional ballerina!" she shouted. She didn't care if the neighbors complained. This was the moment she'd been waiting for!

Alicia said goodbye to her brief musical theater

career and happily turned her focus back to ballet. At SAB, she worked hard to perfect her ballet technique and soon she was invited to join a new dance company called Ballet Caravan. Her career was finally taking off!

Then, in the spring of 1940, Alicia learned that another new dance company, Ballet Theatre, was holding auditions. Alicia decided to try out. To her delight, she was offered a position in the corps de ballet, the big group of "background" dancers in dance companies.

After that, Alicia's career grew quickly. Her life in dance was a whirlwind. At Ballet Theatre, she was given many different roles—first in the corps and then in small ensembles. When she performed in a ballet called *Pas de Quatre* at the Majestic Theater, she and the other three dancers received seventeen curtain calls. *Seventeen!* Alicia could hardly believe it.

Eventually she was asked to dance a solo role

in *Peter and the Wolf* when another ballerina had to drop out at the last minute. Alicia knew this was a huge opportunity for her, and she put everything she had into the part. After that performance, the *New York Times* dance critic John Martin wrote that Alicia "showed herself to be a promising young artist with an easy technique, a fine sense of line and a great deal of youthful charm." Other critics were full of praise for her, too. Alicia wanted to frame those reviews!

The Ballet Theatre choreographers liked to cast Alicia in their dances because she was a gifted actor as well as a skilled ballerina. She was endlessly curious, always seeking the hidden meanings beneath the steps so that she could express those emotions onstage. What was the young swan feeling in *Swan Lake*? What was the bird's motivation in those scenes from *Peter and the Wolf*? What was the spirit's relationship with the other spirits in *Les Sylphides*? Alicia was a true artist, and the choreographers—and the audience—adored her.

When a journalist compared Alicia to a young Anna Pavlova, Alicia thought she would faint from happiness. The future she'd dreamed of was happening right here, right now! Like Pavlova, she'd worked hard to achieve her ambitions. She felt unstoppable!

~

"Look out!"

Alicia heard the warning shout, but it was too late; she bumped into a tall set piece and stumbled backward on the stage. A pair of hands caught her at the last minute before she fell onto the wood floor.

"Thank you," Alicia mumbled, dazed. Sarah, a fellow dancer, was the one who'd grabbed her. Others had stopped dancing, too, and were gathering around her with concerned expressions.

Joanna, the Ballet Theatre stage manager, rushed over.

"Are you all right?"

"I-I'm fine. Really. Just a little slip."

"Do you want to take a break?"

"No. I'm okay. We need to keep rehearsing."

Alicia and the other dancers took their places again. Joanna nodded to the pianist, who resumed playing the music.

But a few bars into the score, in the middle of a pas de bourrée, Alicia collided with another dancer named Dmitri. She hadn't seen him to the left of her.

"I'm so sorry!" Alicia apologized.

Joanna touched Alicia's arm. "Are you *sure* you're all right?" she whispered.

"I thought I was. Perhaps I *should* take a break."

"Why don't you go home and have a proper rest? We can resume in the morning."

Alicia nodded. She grabbed a towel to wipe her

face and headed backstage. Behind her, she could hear the other dancers calling out to her: "Feel better soon!" and "Be well!"

Off the stage and alone, Alicia stopped and blinked once, twice. As she did, little spots floated lazily across her field of vision.

What is happening to me?

The little spots had started a couple of weeks ago. They were like tiny black threads that danced side to side, up and down, always in slow motion. Did they exist *on* her eyeballs? Whenever she looked at herself in the mirror, her eyes appeared perfectly normal. Were they *under* her eyeballs, then?

In the past few days, she'd noticed them worsening, showing up more frequently. She'd noticed, too, that the spots were sometimes accompanied by pops of flashing light. And while she could see straight ahead, she had trouble seeing to the right or left, which was why she kept running into things and people. Her balance was suffering, too, which made spins and turns difficult.

She planned to simply power though the strange sensation to keep dancing, but others disagreed.

"You have to see a doctor," Fernando told her that night.

"I know," Alicia said. "Maybe next week. I'm very busy with rehearsals."

"You should go tomorrow. You're a ballerina. You can't dance if your vision isn't working properly."

Alicia started to protest, then stopped. Fernando was right. She needed healthy eyes in order to dance.

"Fine. I'll try to go tomorrow."

"Don't worry, mi amor. Everything will be fine," Fernando reassured her.

Alicia sighed and nodded. "Okay. But then I'm going right back to rehearsals. And I mean *right* back."

CHAPTER EIGHT

U nfortunately, everything *wasn't* fine, and Alicia wasn't able to go right back to rehearsals. Her doctor had bad news.

"You're suffering from a detached retina in your right eye," he informed her.

"A *what?*"

"The retina is a layer of nerve cells at the back of your eye. The retina in your right eye has become separated from the eye itself. You need an operation to reattach it, or you risk becoming permanently blind."

Permanently blind?

Fernando put his arm around Alicia. "You must have this operation right away. Otherwise..."

"I know," Alicia said, fighting back tears.

Fernando didn't have to spell it out for her. Being blind would surely end Alicia's dance career forever.

Alicia couldn't stand the idea of being in a hospital instead of on the stage. On the other hand, if she *didn't* have the operation, she might never return to the stage again. She could not accept that possibility. Alicia had no other choice. She had to agree to the operation.

Alicia took a brief leave of absence from Ballet Theatre and checked into the hospital. The procedure went well, but it didn't end there. Afterward, she had to stay at the hospital to recover. She lay in the small, cramped bed without moving. The doctors believed that her retina couldn't heal unless she remained completely motionless.

Alicia was desperate to get back to dancing, to her life. And so she mostly obeyed the doctor's instructions to remain perfectly still in her bed. *Mostly.* At times, she would wiggle her feet under the scratchy wool blanket, pointing and stretching. She wanted to keep them in good shape for when she returned to Ballet Theatre.

She eventually did return, but only briefly. Her old symptoms soon came back—the floating spots, the flashing lights, the difficulties with side vision and balance—which sent her back to the hospital for another operation on her eyes.

But the second surgery still didn't solve the problem with her sight. In fact, *both* her retinas required treatment at this point. Alicia's doctor suggested that she return to Havana for another operation. That way, her family and Fernando's family could help out with her recovery, which was likely to last *much* longer than before.

With a heavy heart, Alicia obeyed.

~

"Dance with me, Mamá!"

Alicia woke up to her daughter's sweet voice. In the background, there was music playing on the record player—the score from *Giselle*, which was one of Alicia's favorite ballets.

Alicia started to open her eyes, but there was only darkness. For a moment she'd forgotten that her eyes were still covered with thick bandages from her most recent operation at the hospital in Havana.

"Watch me plié, Mamá!"

"Wonderful, Laurita!" Alicia called out, trying to sound cheerful.

Laura loved to dance, just like her parents. But she was only three, and she didn't understand why her mother couldn't twirl and jump with her.

Alicia's doctors in Havana had ordered her to remain completely motionless for a year. *A year.* She was ordered not to move or cry or even laugh

during that time. Otherwise, doctors worried both retinas might detach again. For a while, weights were even placed on either side of her head so it couldn't shift while she slept.

It was a nightmare. Alicia had become a dancer who couldn't use her body.

Even worse, the doctors told her that after her year in bed was up, she wouldn't be able to return to dance. They said she'd lost too much of her eyesight. They'd declared that her ballet career was over.

Alicia was still so young. How was that possible?

Despair washed over her. She wanted to cry, but she wasn't allowed to do even that.

I'll never dance again, she thought, her chest tightening with anguish. She was like the dying swan in the famous ballet, desperate and broken. Not being able to dance ever again seemed like death to her. Maybe even worse than death...

The bedroom door creaked open.

"Laurita, Abuela has a special treat for you!" It was Fernando.

"A special treat? *Yaaay!*"

With a patter of excited footsteps, Laurita was gone. Alicia a felt weight press down on the edge of the bed as Fernando sat down. He squeezed her hand.

"How are you feeling, mi amor?"

"I feel like dancing."

"I know you do. I'm sorry."

"Will you rehearse with me?"

Fernando hesitated for only a second.

"Yes, of course. Which scene would you like to rehearse today?"

Despite what the doctors had told her, she *hadn't* stopped dancing, not really. She danced in her head. She also danced with her fingers on top of the bed, which she imagined as a stage. Sometimes, Fernando would observe the movements of her fingers and correct her "choreography."

The *Giselle* score was still playing on the record player. Alicia listened carefully.

"*This* scene," she said after a moment. "The act two pas de deux between the ghost of Giselle and Count Albrecht."

"Which part would you like?" Fernando joked.

Alicia had always dreamed of dancing the role
of Giselle.

"Very funny," she said, cracking a small smile.
"Tell me if I get anything wrong, okay? Here we go."

Alicia hummed along with the music for
several bars, to orient herself. Her cue was
coming up soon. As she hummed, she imagined

that she was no longer Alicia Alonso, but the ghost of the peasant girl Giselle. Her lover, Count Albrecht, was kneeling at her grave. He wept as he clasped a bouquet of wilting flowers to his chest. He was full of regret because he had broken her heart, and she had died as a result.

Pain—*Giselle's* pain—coursed through Alicia's motionless body. Also sadness and anger. She began moving her fingertips across the bed. Slowly, slowly. Arabesque en pointe…turn… fifth position…

"To the right," Fernando prompted her in a whisper.

Alicia's fingers pivoted to the right, away from her betrayer, Count Albrecht. They lifted and twirled, twirled and lifted. They felt as real as her actual legs and feet.

The music played on, and Alicia's fingers danced. Once in a while, Fernando would correct her, and she would adjust the choreography accordingly. The delicious smell of stew wafted from the kitchen, but Alicia wasn't hungry. She didn't want to stop dancing. She *never* wanted to stop dancing.

Plié…jeté…pirouette…fouetté…

The music came to a close. "Let's run through it one more time," Alicia told Fernando. "I need to practice for when I dance this role someday."

Fernando didn't correct her or remind her of her diagnosis. He knew her too well. "Yes, of course."

He got up to cue the music. In the darkness behind her bandages, Alicia's mind began dancing again.

She wasn't ready to give up just yet.

CHAPTER NINE

When the long year of recovery was finally over, Alicia expected her vision to be much improved when the bandages came off. But instead, things were almost as bad as before the operations and the many, many months of rest.

Sitting up in bed one morning, she fixed her gaze on her toes peeking out from under the covers. She closed her right eye; her vision out of her left eye was fuzzy but tolerable. She then closed the left eye and opened the right. She could barely see; it was as though she were peering out of glasses with broken, scratched-up lenses.

Keeping her gaze on her toes, she tried to

side-eye the right half of the room. Nothing—just a murky darkness. She tried to the left. A little better, but not by much. Why wasn't her peripheral vision back to normal? Her up-and-down vision wasn't very good, either. It was as though she were seeing everything through a narrow tunnel that stretched ahead of her.

"Be patient," Fernando kept telling her. But it was difficult to be patient when she wanted to be back to 100 percent *now.*

Standing and walking after a year of bed rest was challenging, too. At first, Fernando and Blanca had to help her. They held her arms on either side and moved slowly with her. *Right foot, left foot, right foot, left foot.* It was a frustrating and difficult process, but Alicia pushed through it. She worked as hard at these simple, basic movements as she had at the most advanced ballet technique with her New York City teachers.

Finally, when she was able to walk by herself,

she spoke to her doctor in Havana.

"I'm fine now, right? Not my eyesight, but the rest of me?"

"Well, you're not 'fine,' exactly. You still need to be very careful. You must limit your activities to short walks around the neighborhood. And you must not make any sudden movements. You don't want to risk reinjury to your eyes."

"Of course," Alicia promised.

She had no intention of keeping her promise, though. *I've listened to my doctors long enough,* she thought.

She began taking longer and longer walks every day, sometimes with her Great Dane, Liota. She became used to her bad eyes, and learned to make do—by turning her head when she needed to see sideways and by going out only in the morning and afternoon, when the light was best.

One day, Alicia walked as far as Pro Arte Musical, her old dance school. Wandering through the building, she marveled at how little the place had changed since she and Fernando had moved to New York City. And yet things *had* changed; she knew her brother-in-law, Alberto, had returned from abroad and was running the ballet program there now. He had over a hundred students.

Alicia thought about the early days, when it had been just her and a dozen other girls dancing in street clothes and sneakers. Ballet was finally taking hold in Cuba!

The hallways were empty, although she could hear the sounds of a class upstairs. A female voice was calling out "Plié! Relevé!" over and over again, just like Señor Yavorsky used to do. Wandering around, Alicia found a small unoccupied room with a ballet barre. She went inside and closed the door.

I've missed this so much, she thought wistfully.

Grasping the bar with her right hand, she raised her left leg in the air. Almost immediately,

a sharp pain shot through her left thigh as a muscle cramped up.

"Ow!"

Slumping against the barre, she quickly lowered her leg and massaged the spot. *I need to take it slowly. I'm completely out of shape after a year of not dancing...of not moving at all.*

After that day, Alicia started coming to Pro Arte Musical more and more.

Gradually, she regained her strength, balance, and physical skill, although her eyesight was still a problem. She had to compensate constantly. Alberto invited her to teach at Pro Arte Musical and to perform there, too. Alicia liked being part of the growing ballet scene in Cuba, and so did Fernando; in fact, they'd been talking about opening a ballet school of their own in Havana someday.

But for now, Alicia longed to return to New York City, to Ballet Theatre.

Was she ready? With her limited sight, would she ever be able to dance at her old level again?

~

"Markova is sick. Do you think you can dance *Giselle* in her place?"

Alicia was back at the Ballet Theatre in New York. She blinked at Mr. Dolin, one of the choreographers and principal dancers. She couldn't believe he was asking her to take on the part of Giselle—her dream role!

"You're the only one who knows the part besides Rosella and Nora, and they said they can't get up to speed in so little—"

"Yes! Thank you! I'd love to dance *Giselle!*" Alicia practically shouted. She couldn't possibly turn down such an extraordinary opportunity.

Mr. Dolin nodded. "Good. You can start rehearsals right away. We only have five days before the performance."

Five days?

Since she had moved back to New York City a month ago, the Ballet Theatre had welcomed her with open arms. She'd already performed in a few smaller ballets, and they'd figured out how to accommodate her vision issues. The stage crew would shine bright spotlights or flashlights to direct her movements and to keep her from accidentally dancing off the stage or falling into the orchestra pit. The other dancers would subtly touch her arm or back to guide her this way or that, or whisper instructions in her ear.

As Mr. Dolin walked away, Alicia leaned against the stage door, her face flushed and her heart pounding like crazy. She was beyond excited—but also a little terrified. What had she just agreed to? She'd never danced *Giselle* before, other than with her fingertips during her long recovery in Havana. Fingertip-dancing wasn't the same as real dancing on a real stage with real dancers. She'd have to compress five weeks of rehearsal into five days.

You can do it, Alicia, she told herself. She'd overcome bigger obstacles before.

And so she began working nonstop with Mr. Dolin to learn her steps and rehearse with him. She barely took breaks to sleep and eat.

On the evening of the performance, the Metropolitan Opera House was filled to capacity. The audience, who'd expected to see the famous Alicia Markova as Giselle, was curious to see how the young substitute, Alicia Alonso, would fill the prima ballerina's shoes. In her dressing room, Alicia tied the ribbons of her pointe shoes and checked and rechecked her makeup, hoping she wouldn't disappoint anyone.

And she didn't. That night, Alicia became Giselle, just as she'd become Giselle in Havana while lying in bed with her eyes covered in bandages. Through her graceful movements, she

conveyed the young peasant girl's fragility and her love for Count Albrecht, drawing inspiration from her memories of first falling in love with Fernando. In act two, she radiated pain and anguish as Count Albrecht wept at her grave; for this, she drew inspiration from how she'd felt when the doctors had told her she would never be able to dance again.

After the finale, the audience burst into applause. They clapped and cheered and called out Alicia's name. They threw bouquets on the stage and shouted "Brava!" over and over again.

Alicia's eyes filled with happy tears as she curtsied once, twice, three times. She gazed out at the crowd, who were on their feet now. They looked like fuzzy, blurry shadows to her, but she didn't care. She'd made it. She truly *was* unstoppable.

CHAPTER TEN

A fter *Giselle,* Alicia's fame continued to grow. Dance critics gave her rave reviews. The Ballet Theatre choreographers offered her more and more parts.

In 1944, she was photographed for *Life,* which was one of the most well-known and popular magazines of the time. Soon after that edition was published, she received a letter from her mother:

Mijita,

Papá and I saw you in the Cuban edition of Life *magazine. We were so surprised! We knew you had been working hard to become a professional ballerina in America. But you didn't tell us that you are so famous!*

I want you to know that Papá bought every copy he could find in Havana and gave them to all our friends and relatives.

We are so proud of you.

Con cariño,
Mamá

The letter made Alicia happier than all the applause and standing ovations and rave reviews combined. Papá had never approved of her becoming a dancer, but now he was bragging about it to his friends.

Everything had turned out well after all.

~

"Plié…relevé…plié…relevé!" Alicia called out. "Straighten those legs! Hold in your stomachs! Necks up, shoulders down!"

Alicia walked around the studio of her new

dance school, Academia Nacional de Ballet
Alicia Alonso, clapping to the music as her young
students ran through their warm-ups. They
wore leotards and tights and ballet slippers,
and their hair was neatly tied or combed back.
They watched Alicia carefully and even a little
nervously as she inspected their movements. She
knew they were eager to please their teacher,
just like she'd always been eager to please *her*
teachers. Alicia's studio was just as strict as Señor
Yavorsky's had been.

In 1950, Alicia and Fernando had fulfilled
their longtime dream of opening a school for
ballet in Havana. They wanted to give back to
their community, to their country, by helping to
nurture the next generation of ballet dancers.

They based themselves in Havana, but they
couldn't give up touring and performing completely.
They still made trips to New York City to dance
with Ballet Theatre, which had been renamed

American Ballet Theatre, and with other ballet companies, too. They also brought their dancer friends back to Havana with them to teach and perform.

Fernando's brother, Alberto, was part of the school, too. Over the years, Alberto had become one of the most important dancers, teachers, and choreographers in Cuba.

In fact, Alicia and Fernando and Alberto had also created a professional Cuban ballet company together—Ballet Alicia Alonso. It was still a young organization with very little money or other resources. But it was growing. And Alicia's school would help train future ballet dancers to join the company.

An hour later, Alicia dismissed her class. The students scattered to collect their bags and other belongings. They waved goodbye to her as they headed for the door.

"Don't forget about *Coppélia* rehearsals

tomorrow at ten!" she reminded them.

"Yes, Señora Alonso!"

"Mamá!"

Laurita—now Laura, since she wasn't such a little girl anymore—pranced up to Alicia with a big smile on her face. She wore a leotard, pink tights, and pink ballet shoes. With her long hair pulled back in a ponytail and her large brown eyes, she looked like a younger version of her mother.

"What is it, mijita?" Alicia asked her.

"Can you show me the brisé en avant again? I can't seem to get it quite right."

"Yes, of course! Here, let's start with the demi-plié in fifth position. Now brush your back leg forward through first position, then to the front..."

Laura was one of Alicia's best students. In class, Alicia tried not to give her daughter special treatment, but it was difficult; she wanted to cheer every time Laura soared through the air in a joyful grand jeté or spun around and around in a neat, precise pirouette.

"Now spring forward!"

And Laura sprang.

"That was exactly right," Alicia said, beaming. "Since I have you here all to myself, would you like me to teach you a brisé en arrière? Going backward, not forward?"

"Yes, please!"

Alicia demonstrated the step, and Laura followed. As they worked together, Alicia wondered if her lovely, talented daughter would become a professional dancer like herself and Fernando. She thought so. She hoped so. Laura and the other students at the Academia Nacional de Ballet Alicia Alonso were the future of dance in Cuba. Alicia had been there in the very beginning. She was proud and honored that she was here now to help see it through.

Alicia Alonso continued running her ballet company and school for many decades. She also continued performing, not only in Cuba and the United States but all over the world, and she choreographed dances, too. She did all this despite the fact that her eyesight grew even worse over the years. Further operations would help her for a time, but then her vision would deteriorate again. There were times she couldn't see well enough to walk onto the stage.

And still, she pushed forward with her hallmark work ethic and tenacity. She didn't want her vision to be an issue for her audience. "I can accept my blindness. I don't want my audience thinking that if I dance badly, it is because of my eyes. Or if I dance well, it is in spite of them. This is not how an artist should be," she said in 1971.

Audiences all over the world loved her—for

her passion, dedication, incredible technique, and exquisite interpretations. They also loved her for her range; she was able to bring beauty and truth to a wide variety of roles: old and new, classical and modern, Cuban and non Cuban, Western and non-Western. Her repertoire included everything from *Giselle* and *Carmen* and the *Nutcracker* to nonstory ballets like *Theme and Variations*, which George Balanchine created for her and her dance partner Igor Youskevitch in 1947.

Cuba underwent great social and political upheaval in the second half of the twentieth century. As a result, the US and Cuba cut off diplomatic, trade, and other ties with each other for a long time. Many people were angry that Alicia returned to Cuba and seemed to align herself with Fidel Castro's communist government. But through her performances, Alicia has also been credited with helping to ease tensions between the two countries in her own small way. She also managed to keep her dance company and school going through these difficult times. Today, Ballet Alicia Alonso—now called Ballet Nacional de Cuba—is one of the most important dance companies internationally, and its school is the largest ballet school in the world.

Despite their artistic partnership, Alicia and Fernando had problems later on in their marriage, and so they divorced in the mid-1970s. Soon after, she married Pedro Simón, a dance critic. In 1995, at seventy-four years old, Alicia danced her last ballet performance: *Farfalla*, a butterfly-themed dance that she choreographed. She received many awards and honors before and after her retirement as a ballerina.

Alicia passed away on October 17, 2019, at the age of ninety-eight. She remained involved in the world of ballet well into her nineties and left behind a legacy of stunning choreography, as well as a generation of dancers who continue to dazzle.

Laura Alonso followed in her mother's footsteps and became a prominent ballerina and teacher. After dancing with the Ballet Nacional de Cuba for twenty-five years, she went on to dance with other companies around the world. Today, she continues to work with London's Royal Ballet School, the Danish Royal Ballet, and other renowned schools and companies.

CLAIM YOUR SPACE

Alicia was a powerful presence on stage, drawing the audience's eyes to her as they followed her expressive and emotional performances. She loved how the fierce, confident rhythm of the music made her feel fierce and confident in turn (page 22). It gave her strength to take up space on the stage, which inspired her to take up space in the world. You can do this, too! Use your body to make a few simple shapes and see how strong it makes you feel.

- See how far you can you stretch your body.
- Try to take up as much space as possible without moving your feet.
- Try to take up as much space as possible using a movement that travels through space, such as skipping, running, crawling, etc.

NOW LET'S PUT SOME EMOTION INTO IT!

- Make a full-body shape that makes you feel COMFORTABLE.
- Make a full-body shape that makes you feel SCARED.
- Make a full-body shape that makes you feel CONFIDENT.

How did it make you feel to move through these emotions with your body? How do you think this activity can translate into your everyday life?

COORDINATE YOUR MOVEMENTS

Training your brain to multitask can be useful both in dance and in real life. When learning to play the castanets, Alicia had to move her hands and feet in different ways at the same time (page 23). You can combine hand gestures with foot movements, too. Improve your own coordination with the following steps.

1. Create three movements with just your hands or arms.

   • Shake your hands like you're drying them out in front of you.
   • Draw a rainbow with your arms above your head.
   • Pretend you're playing the castanets like Alicia: raise your arms in the air and tap your middle, ring, and pinky fingers against your palms.

2. Try all three hand movements in a row.

3. Now try performing your hand movements while walking forward, then walking backward.

4. Try the same gestures while turning, walking on the low level (close to the ground) or high level (tiptoes or jumping).

What was the most challenging part of this exercise? What was the most fun? What did you learn about your own coordination?

MAKE BALLET YOUR OWN

Alicia perfected the art of ballet through years of training and dedication. She understood that a dancer must know all the fundamentals before learning how to make the dance her own. Let's learn some of Alicia's signature ballet moves so you can make them your own, too. Remember that practice makes perfect, and as Alicia told herself on page 101, "You can do it"!

Try out these three ballet technique positions:

Plié
Stand tall with straight legs and bring your heels together and toes apart to a first position. Start bending your knees while keeping your heels on the ground and posture straight. Then straighten your knees to your starting position.

Arabesque

Standing on your right leg, extend your left leg behind you while your torso bends forward slightly. The leg behind you is straight, and toes are pointed. Extend your left arm out to the side and right arm out in front of you for balance. Now try the other side.

Pirouette

"Pirouette" is a French word that means "to twirl." Starting on two feet, start with a "plié" and try to make a full turn while balancing on your right leg. Your standing (right) leg is straight and your left toes touch your ankle or knee as you spin around.

Once you've mastered these positions, you can create your own versions that are unique to you.

- Try these positions using different body parts.
- Now try them on the low level or the high level.
- Explore moving in and out of these positions.

How did it make you feel to take ownership of these steps and create something all your own?

Now that you've learned how to take up space, improve your coordination, and practice your technique, it's time for you to choreograph your own dance! Using the movements you practiced, come up with a dance routine that is uniquely YOU. Share it with your friends and family the way Alicia did with hers.

SMASHWORKS DANCE

Smashworks Dance is a New York–based dance company founded and directed by choreographer Ashley McQueen. We dance to advocate for human rights issues and women's empowerment through performing arts, educational programming, and community outreach. We make dance accessible and inspire audiences to take action through our performances both onstage and in site-specific environments. We view artistic expression as power—*smashing* stereotypes and promoting dance as a unifying and confidence-building practice for all.

Visit Smashworks Dance at smashworksdance.com
Facebook (Facebook.com/smashworksdance)
Instagram (@smashworksdance)

ACKNOWLEDGMENTS

Nothing could stop Alicia Alonso from dancing. Her spirit reminds us to persevere in the face of adversity, to recognize the importance of working together in an ensemble, and to champion the global impact of women's artistic achievements.

Nancy Ohlin, you deserve a standing ovation for dazzling readers with such an enchanting narrative. Josefina Preumayr, thank you for your illustrations, which flow so gracefully on the page. Thank you, too, to Martha Cipolla and Marisa Finkelstein for copyediting and proofreading with such care and attention to detail.

To Smashworks Dance, you're absolute stars. This partnership and collaboration have been such a blast. Thank you, Ashley McQueen and Ana Lejava, for your creativity, commitment, and excitement around this project.

And, finally, thank you to our Rebel Girls readers. Your perpetual curiosity keeps us on our toes! Have the courage to perfect your craft, and dance toward your dreams. The world is your stage.

ABOUT REBEL GIRLS

REBEL GIRLS is an award-winning cultural media engine founded in 2012, spanning over 70 countries. Rebel Girls is on a mission to empower a generation of inspired and confident girls through diverse stories that resonate with audiences of all ages, celebrating women's accomplishments and pursuits across history, geography, and field. This diverse and passionate group of rebels works in Los Angeles, New York, Atlanta, Merida, London, and Milan.